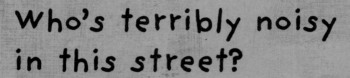
Who's terribly noisy
in this street?

Stories and rhymes in this book

VISITORS

HAPPY HOLIDAYS

IMAGINE!

MRS PARRY'S PARROT

INVITATION

D.I.Y. TIGERS

ROADSIDE REPAIRS

ANOTHER NOISY NIGHT

A TIGER LULLABY

A catalogue record for this book is available from the British Library

Published by Ladybird Books Ltd
27 Wrights Lane London W8 5TZ
A Penguin Company
© LADYBIRD BOOKS LTD MCMXCIX

Produced for Ladybird Books Ltd by Nicola Baxter and Amanda Hawkes

The Terrible Tigers

by Joan Stimson

illustrated by Eric Smith

Ladybird

VISITORS

They rev up their truck.
They roar round the bend.

They toot
on the horn,
When they
see a friend.

They screech to a halt
In front of your gate.
It's the Terrible Tigers
From Seventy-Eight!

HAPPY HOLIDAYS

The Terrible Tigers were
going camping. And they'd
asked Grandma and Grandad
to petsit.

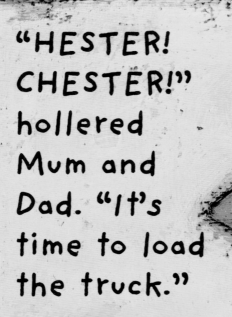

"HESTER!
CHESTER!"
hollered
Mum and
Dad. "It's
time to load
the truck."

"What a din!" said the
neighbours. "But at least,"
they told each other...

"those Terrible Tigers
will be gone soon. Then
WE can have a holiday
from all that noise!"

Next morning
the Terrible
Tigers looked
out eagerly
for Grandma
and Grandad.

And so
did the
neighbours.

"I think
I can hear
them,"
smiled
Hester.

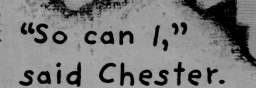

"So can I,"
said Chester.

NEENA! NEENA! Grandma
was sounding the siren on
their old police van.

And a few minutes later...

BOING! BOING! BOING!
Grandad bounced out of the
van with his new drum kit.

"Oh, no," groaned the
neighbours. "No holiday
for us after all."

But then one of them had a brainwave. "Why don't you go camping, too?" they asked Grandma and Grandad. "WE'LL look after the pets!"

It was a TERRIBLY good idea!

IMAGINE!

I can be a tractor.

I can be a train.

I can be a stripey bus.

I can be
a plane.

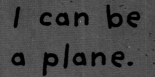

I can be a
digger.
(What a load
I've got!)

I can be myself as well...
The loudest of the lot!

MRS PARRY'S PARROT

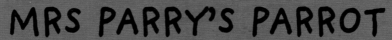

Old Mrs Parry had lost her parrot.

"Has anyone seen little Sydney?" she asked the neighbours.

But at number
seventy-eight,
she couldn't
make anyone
hear. She
knocked...

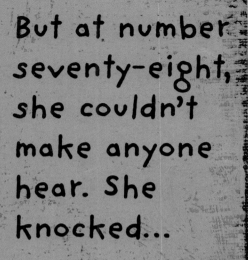

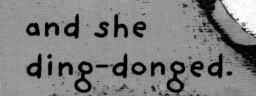
and she
ding-donged.

She shouted and called until
she was exhausted.

But there was no reply. The Terrible Tigers were making so much noise...

they couldn't hear her.

When Hester and Chester came out at last, they fell over Mrs Parry on the doorstep.

"I've lost Sydney," she sobbed. "And now I'm too tired to look for him."

"PARROT ALERT! PARROT ALERT!" shouted the cubs...

running up and down the streets.

And before Mrs Parry
had drunk her tea...

little Sydney had been
found and was finishing
her biscuit.

INVITATION

There are nibbles and nuggets.

There are sauces and dips.

There's burping, and slurping,

And smacking of lips.

There's
swooping,

And
whooping,

Those tigers can't wait.

"PLEASE come and join us,
This picnic is great!"

D.I.Y. TIGERS

The Terrible Tigers were making even more noise than usual.

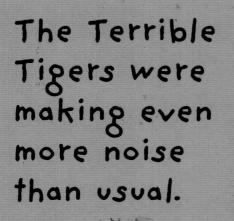

"We're doing up our truck," they told the neighbours proudly.

There were whoops as
Mum and Dad whizzed
round with the sandpaper.

There were shrieks as
Hester and Chester flew
round with the filler.

But for once the neighbours didn't mind.

"No more looking at that rusty old wreck," they said.

Then they all went to bed early and put their heads under their pillows.

The Terrible Tigers banged about late into the evening.

"At last!" said Dad. "We've finished the undercoat."

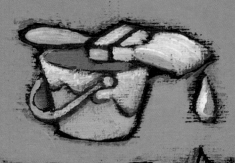

"When will it be dry?" asked the cubs.

"In exactly eight hours," said Mum.

So at first light, the Terrible Tigers bounced back outside and tackled the top coat.

"Isn't it BRILLIANT?" they yelled, when the neighbours pulled back their curtains.

"It certainly is," groaned the neighbours, as they dived for their sunglasses!

ANOTHER NOISY NIGHT

The Terrible Tigers sent all their neighbours an invitation.

Enjoy an evening of exciting entertainment! And help raise cash for sick cubs.

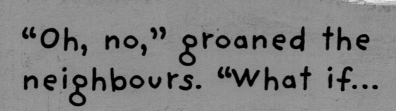

"Oh, no," groaned the neighbours. "What if...

those tigers
do their
terrible
magic tricks?

Or tell their
terrible
jokes?"

But they agreed, "We must
help the sick cubs. So we'll
have to go."

On the evening of the entertainment, the neighbours dragged their paws as they padded along to number seventy-eight.

Suddenly, one of them had a DREADFUL thought...

But Mum and Dad were already flinging open the door.

"Welcome to our try-it-yourself tap dancing spectacular!" they boomed.

The neighbours looked at each other. It was going to be TERRIBLY noisy!

But at the end of the evening, they all agreed...

It was
TERRIBLY
GOOD FUN,
too!

A TIGER LULLABY

Sleep tight, tired tigers,

May sweet
dreams come
your way.

Then wake
up fresh
tomorrow...

To another NOISY DAY!